A DREAM PREMONITION IN A LIFE LESS ORDINARY

By

Patricia Bailey

ISBN 978-1-84753-758-4

A DREAM PREMONITION IN A LIFE LESS ORDINARY

Chapters

FOREWORD

A simple tribute to an outstanding son of Liverpool.

Even though it is true to say in 1968 that Liverpool was awash with talent and greatness, Stuart Duncan Howitt stood out with his good looks, sophistication and talent. Stu Howitt was a one-off with his rarity of uniqueness, phenomenally so. At that time in Liverpool's rich history Stu Howitt was right up there with Liverpool's finest sons. The best of best!

A brave courageous champion, sophisticated and true with a gentleness of a real gentleman, a genuine man, he was rich in every sense of the word!!

The late Stu Howitt was all of these things and much more, who has enriched my extremely difficult life for nearly forty years. Our paths crossed many times in those fabulous years when Liverpool was at its best which the history books will show, in Liverpool's rich history that you and I, Stu, were part of.

This is my attempt of giving Stu Howitt something back for all the respect and tenderness that he gave to me all those years ago, with a great expectation of a lifelong love affair to follow. But I never had a Future, just a date with Destiny. Tomorrow is promised to no one –

Stu on one of his Speed-boats in 1967

CHAPTER ONE
FOOTPRINTS

Today, Monday the 15th of May 2006 should have been a celebration for Stuart Duncan Howitt's 64th birthday. Born the same year as that world famous, hugely talented son of Liverpool, Paul McCartney, Stu Howitt went to the same school, as John Lennon, Quarry Bank Grammar. Stu Howitt was in the same league as John Lennon and Paul McCartney, in every sense of the word, they were his peers.

The first born to Olive and Joseph Howitt in 1942, in the Walton suburb of Liverpool. Stu was twelve years older than his younger brother Andrew, and fifteen years older than their baby brother Jonathan Howitt, and their mum's great pride and joy, especially Stuart, being an only child for twelve years. Stu Howitt was to become "The Great Love of my Life" some twenty six years later in Liverpool, in January 1968.

Stu was seven years older than me and astrologically speaking we were the perfect personality match, both of us being born under Earth, Sun signs, of Taurus and Virgo with compatibility numerological life path numbers in harmony. Stu's memory is still so fresh in my mind's eye, so vivid, some thirty-eight years later.

I was eighteen when I first met this charismatic of champions of the car-racing circuit and champion water-skier. There is no doubt in my mind that Stu would go on to become world champion. That's who he was. His memory and impact on my life haunt me still, and will no doubt continue to affect me for the rest of my life. "The Love of my Life," a love so deep, buried deep down inside of me forever!! Sometimes in life we are blessed with a rare opportunity to meet the most unique and charismatic of individuals, who cross our paths so briefly like "Footprints in the Sand." Washed away with the oncoming tide, lost forever but who remain imprinted on our hearts and minds for eternity.

I have yet to meet someone to compare with his greatness and serene, gentle affectionate nature, even all these years later. Stu was pure platinum who could easily have outshone the most sophisticated, glamorous, Golden Boys of the sixties without even trying, and he did! There was a great abundance of extraordinarily talented, good-looking boys around on the music scene, in films and in the world of sport at that time throughout the country, as well as in my home town, but especially in Liverpool in 1968. Paul McCartney, The Searchers, Billy J Kramer, and in the world of sport George Best, half of the Everton Football Club, Colin Harvey. Not forgetting the actors Terence Stamp, Albert Finney and Michael Caine. The list was endless all over the country as the swinging sixties progressed.

According to Eastern Astrology, my beloved Stuart was born in the year of the Horse. A magnificent blue/black haired thoroughbred if ever there was one! A truly magnificent champion in every way, hallelujah! How lucky can you be? He had it ALL and then some. Impeccably dressed, so elegant, with the softest, gentlest of voices. He adored his mother, who had a similar nature to her oldest son, Stuart, who must have been such a great comfort to her during the war years in Liverpool. Olive Howitt's first born had a hearing defect as a child, which, I'm certain, gave Stuart an inner strength and sensitive awareness of others who felt somewhat different and apart. As a result he developed a steel-like determination to succeed throughout his short life span. A Winner, a Leader, Brave and Courageous. Like the astrological symbol of the Chinese astrological sign of the Horse that he was born under. Exactly the same qualities and strengths. Combined with the traits of a true to type Taurean, calm, steadfast, down to earth, he was simply "The Best of the Best".

The Howitt family business was really rocketing after Stu started working at their import and export company on Derby Road at Liverpool's Pier Head. Stuart ran the transport side of the business and he had his own "Pit Stop" garage right next door which his younger brother Andrew worked at for some extra pocket money during his school holidays and weekends. As a little boy Stuart attended Florence Melly Primary School on Walton Road and later Quarry Bank. John Lennon originally named his first Pop Group after Quarry bank, the Quarrymen, at that time, in Liverpool's rich history.

It was during this stage in his life that his family, whilst living at 308 Queen's Drive, Walton, that the Howitts owned a bicycle shop at Cherry Lane, which as a child I visited with my Grandmother Minnie Jackson, my father's mother. My dad was an only child, so I always visited my Grandmother on Sundays and Wednesdays at 49 Maiden Lane, being the only granddaughter and first grandchild. That's when I got to visit the Cherry Lane area of Liverpool. Strangely enough I remember gazing into a bike shop window as a child. The bike shop was owned by the Howitts, as I was to discover thirty-seven years later.

Two-wheeler bikes were top of my agenda from seven years onwards. It was on another bicycle window-shopping expedition one Sunday morning after 11 o'clock Sunday morning Mass, at St Michael's RC Church, West Derby Road, with my other Grandmother Sarah Joyce, whom I was so privileged to have spent twenty years of my life with from about the age of four, right up to November, 25th 1974 when my magnificent Nan died, at only sixty-six years of age.

During the sixties, Liverpool was the most religious city in Europe, I remember this Sunday morning oh so well! It was in July, a hot summer's morning. This day would become a day I would remember my whole life through. My wonderful Nan and I were dressed for church. My Nan would always wear her black satin Parisian Pill-Box hat with matching coat and accessories and I would wear one of the many beautiful dresses that my Nan designed an had made for me. I was a tiny little thing with short blonde hair tied up in a big bow on the side of my head, sparkling white shoes and ankle socks, proud as punch to be out walking with my beloved Grandmother who looked like my mother.

My Nan had no resemblance to a Grandmotherly type whatsoever - she was extremely good-looking lady with a creative style for interior design and acute business acumen, but it was her huge, generous nature and fantastic wit and sense of humour that were her greatest attributes that warmed people to her. For twenty years of my life I was able to draw from the Well of Wisdom of Life from my Grandmother's great awareness and experiences of life. My Nan, it always felt to me, had lived three lifetimes in her sixty-six years of life. I knew, for about two years before my Nan died, that she would leave me within that time span.

Getting back to that Sunday morning in July 1957, after Sunday morning mass walking down West Derby Road we passed by Sharples Bike Shop. Mr Sharples was working in his shop. As we passed by I had just about convinced my Nan that I had been able to ride a two-wheeler bike, in the hopeful expectation of receiving a bike for my eighth birthday the following month in August. We stopped to look at the collection of two-wheelers in Sharples window display when I could hardly believe my ears! My wonderful Nan suddenly asked me, but totally in character asked me right out loud which bike did I want. That one! There on the top rack in the display. "The Blue Rudge, that one, Nan" I answered in haste.

My Nan walked to the opened doorway and directly instructed Mr Sharples to take the "Blue Rudge" down from the window and that we would collect it the following morning and that it was to be my birthday present, for my 8th birthday.

What a magnanimous person, that was my Nan. Boy, did I treasure that bike. Unfortunately it took me a few days to learn to ride, covered in bruises, but I could ride that bike. No way would I let my beloved Nan down. Boy did I always love my Nan like there was no tomorrow and I still do. But this tremendous act of generosity has given me such joy and happiness whenever I remember in my mind's eye that prolific Sunday in July 1957.

I suspect my own psychic awareness was greatly developed through both my Grandmother's and mother's sensitive sensibility, and awareness. In particular it was shortly after moving back to Shiel Park from living out at Hunt's Cross for five and a half years, from the end of December 1967 through the beginning of 68, when I was just 18 and keen to hear what was going to happen in my life that I would pester my Grandmother to give me a card reading with the playing cards and tea leaves. That became one of the most accurate of readings I have ever had in my life hitherto. The reading was always the same during the first few months of 1968. The cards would always turn up with a car accident with a death of a Jack of Spades and there would be a Queen of Spades and King of Spades involved in this tragedy although it didn't register with me at that time, the run-up to Stu Howitt's untimely tragic accident that it could have anything to do with Stuart.

But on the 15th June 1968 at Oulton Park Race Track Stu Howitt was DEAD. Stu was somersaulted three times after hitting the bank and landing upside down into "Knickerbrook" sucked down into the mud for over half an hour in his white Hillman Imp number thirty-seven in the race. It is my understanding that had the race officials acted promptly Stu would more than likely still be here. Andrew Howitt assures me that the car was still in tact, only covered in mud. Stuart Howitt had choked on a false tooth and that's what killed him! Oulton Park Race Track named a race after my beloved Stuart.

Many years later I would get to visit Oulton Park Race Track with the Late Peter Bailey one August Bank Holiday Monday shortly after my marriage to Bailey in 1977. It was only a few short weeks before Stu,s fatal accident, at Oulton Park Race Track, that he acquired a Licence to race for the British Car Racing Tournament ,with a sponsorship from Castrol Oil and Redex.. Speed and danger were his great passion.

Howitts Bike Shop in Cherry Lane, 1961, Liverpool

CHAPTER TWO
BIKES

Whilst living with my Grandmother at 42 Lavan Street in Liverpool between the age of four or five years old, I remember having a dream which I found to be a fearful experience at that time. I kept remembering this dream week's later; unable to talk about this frightening feeling whenever I recalled the dream. Being a highly reserved and excruciatingly painfully shy little creature, I was rather stoic and quiet as a child, who wouldn't cry or show my feelings in front of anyone. But with a "hell of a temper," stubborn and independent and extremely aware of my mother's anxieties and unhappiness from a very earlier age. My mum would always talk to me about the problems and the situation with my father's problems with unemployment and anger and general "warring" going on in the family.

My Nan never wanted my highly talented good-looking mother to marry my father, and likewise my father's mother did not want my dad an only child to marry my mother. This continued right up to my Nan's death in 1974. It was only when my Granddad died that the reason for the verbal abuse that he had always given to my dad was on account of Granddad's having to marry my Grandmother Minnie because she was pregnant with my dad; this transpired when we discovered the marriage certificate. On his death on the 27th November 1974 my Granddad was seventy-four years of age.

The truth be told, my mother was far too intelligent and talented to be married especially to someone like my Scouse git of a part-time father. But to be fair my father had been emotionally abused all his life by *his* father, John Jackson. My Granddad John Jackson died in the same hospital, Newsham General, as my beloved Nan Sarah Joyce, they died within twenty-four hours of each other. Granddad died first, on Sunday 24th November 1974, and my Nan at 12.30 am on the 25th November 1974.

What a year 1974 turned out to be. My mother had to have two throat operations in May 1974 and September 1974. Each time my poor mum couldn't speak for months after each operation, which was unbearable for someone like my mum who loves to talk. I had severe food poisoning and had been vomiting blood and had to be taken to hospital. I was so ill for weeks later. And then my Granddad was taken into hospital and then my poor Nan. We had to attend two funerals in one week, unbelievably tragic, gigantic stress and trauma.

From the age of eight to thirteen years I lived with my Nan and Step-Granddad in Shiel Park. I remember distinctly riding my new 21" lilac and purple coloured new bike on which my feet just barely touched the pedals and how the other kids would taunt me because the bike was a bit too big for me, but I grew into it. That was another expensive gift for my 12th birthday from my wonderful Nan. My Nan was the best. It was always my Nan who fought for me at school with the Nuns, or defended me, throughout twenty-four years of my life with anyone and everyone who gave me a hard time. You see the privileges; I had been able to experience such loyalty and support, throughout all the traumatic and warring years.

One day during the summer six week break from school in 1961 I was riding back home from visiting my mum and dad and my brother Kenny one sunny afternoon down Boaler Street. Boaler Street had for many years featured in our family history when my mother would roller-skate down that smooth straight road. In her childhood and throughout her Life, my mother was a prolific skater, dancer, singer, swimmer, with a compassionate warm friendly nature. My father's Aunty Lilly had a general mini market shop on the corner of Shiel Park. Boaler Street which ran parallel, to West Derby Road. At ten years of age I would work in my Great Aunty Lilly's mini market, stacking shelves and dressing the windows for extra pocket money. After school two evenings a week (for 25 pence a week).

I was just about to ride into the side entrance of Shiel Park, when I decided to cycle onto the pavement into the gated entrance of Shiel Park, when I noticed a young man standing a few feet at the side of what was a former cinema which used to be called "The Cosy" but it was now a show room for cabin cruisers and speed boats. I remember vividly that look, there was no mistaking that long, lingering look between the two of us. It took me thirty-seven years to discover the reason why this deep lasting memory stayed with me, the look so different and intimate. He was smiling at the thought of my determination of riding the 21" frame bike which meant so much to me. A 21" frame cycle for such a little girl, and because of his love of bikes from their former cycle shop drew his attention towards me as I cycled past him.

THIS WAS THE FIRST TIME I SAW STUART DUNCAN HOWITT. Some six years later this would be the exact spot where Stu would always collect me to go out on a date, just a few feet away from my Aunty Lilly's shop, at the opposite end of the block from the former Cosy cinema. It would be many years later until I got to see him again. It was shortly after moving back to Shiel Park from Hunt's Cross, where George Harrison (one of the Beatles) lived at 174 Macketts Lane, whom could be seen driving his dark green Jag on a good day.

In fact in just a matter of weeks I had found a job in an office in the prolific Corn Exchange building in Liverpool's business city centre, in December 1967. When Stu Howitt walked in for the Bills of Lading in Frank Strick's Import and Export office I felt so uncomfortable with being new and so shy and self conscious and insecure, sitting at my desk directly behind the large reception desk. I was, as Stu would later tell me, very pretty. Pretty enough to have my picture in the Liverpool Echo as a good-looking daughter of Liverpool. The Liverpool Echo would publish photographs of the local girls on a daily basis at that time during the sixties. The problem was I didn't have any photos, it was an imposition having my photograph taken back then, I was so critical of myself and still am, I am very much a Virgoan, highly critical of myself. Each time I would look up, Stu was looking at me smiling but I didn't smile back, too shy.

Unfortunately the job didn't last too long. A few weeks later, in January 1968, I got myself a job at the "Cabin Club" in Wood Street which is still up and running today. At that time it was a casino-cum-nightclub. I was going to be the "Cook from the Cabin". I would cook and serve food, cash up, and give the order for supplies for three nights a week. I got the job after responding to an advertisement in the Liverpool Echo, for Cloak rooms Hat check Girl. Funny, how things turnout! I didn't reply to the first Advert, I lost my nerve. Too afraid of rejection, then a second advert, a couple of weeks, later appeared, in the Echo. Somehow, I managed to summon up the courage to telephone; I was given the job, as the Cook from the Cabin, after being interviewed, by the two Partners, Brian and Ian. Who insisted that I start working for them right then and there, which, I did. Little did I know that this was the Club that Stuart had his 21 Birthday party, just, a few years earlier. This was Stu Howitts, club. My date with DESTINY!

It was at the Cabin within days of working at the club that Stu Howitt walked in with his General Manager, Wally Browne and two girls whom I recognized from the Liverpool scene at that time, the girls came from extremely wealthy families. He recognized me immediately, as I did him, from Frank Strick's office just a few weeks earlier. I took their order from Stu and he added that he wanted the bill and oh would you put your phone number on the back of the bill? Yes, I answered, to the amazement of his companions. They must have wondered what was going on. Who the hell was I? How did Stu know me?

A couple of weeks went by, no call, then, Stu came in to the Cabin again, still promising to call. Another few weeks went by and nothing. Then on Saturday 10th February 1968 he walked in by himself. Oh god, did he look gorgeous or what! You bet he did. He was wearing a beautiful beige suede jacket, black Gucci shoes – not many people in Liverpool in 1968 even knew of Gucci, let alone owned a pair of Gucci shoes – pink shirt and his gold Omega watch, 6 foot 2 inches tall with the bluest black hair I have ever seen in my entire life. Walking straight up to me informing me that he had "come in for me". I explained that I had to work till 02.30 am. That's alright, he said, I will wait. Oh my god did I get lucky. We walked to his dad's Mark 10 Jaguar in Berry Street. Oh! How I loved the way we would glide around in that Jag, it was seventh heaven away from all the realities of my life and family, the never-ending money worries and tyrannical father, "warring family" and my terminally ill beloved Nan who could hardly breathe. It broke my heart to see my Nan suffering and still listening and helping everyone, that was my Nan, although I never referred to any of these problems to Stuart, how could I? If I were to go on seeing him, I dare not mention at that time the reality of my life situation, nor did I admit to living in Shiel

Park, I pretended I was just staying with a relative, and that I lived at Hunt's Cross which was a wealthier area of Liverpool.

We drove around Allerton and Queen's Drive, eventually we stopped in Penny Lane, Stu needed to use the public lavatory in penny Lane. We then drove to a well known spot for lovers, Otterspool Promenade. He stopped the car. Stu then shouted very assertively: "Now I've got you!" He stated that he was sure I was a virgin. I was, and I intended to stay that way for some considerable time, and I had no intention of becoming pregnant at eighteen and a half years of age. Nor, I had decided, was I going to lose my virginity until I was at least twenty one or twenty two. I had no intention of bringing any trouble to my Nan or Mum. My family would never have given up on the situation, my whole life long. I couldn't let them down; they had made sacrifices for me and my brother, so it was my way of giving them something back for all the love and sacrifices that they had made all of my life.

Stu was so affectionate and loving towards me, so serene, so sensuous, this was the first time I had ever stayed out all night. I had enormous difficulty getting out of his dad's car on that Sunday morning at 8.30 am. I couldn't bear to leave him; I must have had foreboding about him .Right then and there. I just wanted to stay with him forever! The red-haired paper boy was just completing his round as I got to the front door of my Nan's apartment at 176 Pendine Close, Shiel Park. Stu asked me to go out on the Tuesday for a drink. I desperately wanted to be with him later that day. But he was taking his two younger brothers to Chester Zoo on that Sunday. Tuesday 13th February couldn't come quickly enough. Monday the 12th February I went to the best shopping street. Bold St in Liverpool was at that time the equivalent to Old Bond Street in London, and I bought a Marquisette tortoiseshell hair-slide and some "Tabu" cologne for my big date with Stu on Tuesday night. From Hills Hair dressers. Stuart rang to confirm our date on Monday night and I explained it was difficult with business commitments to plan ahead with any arrangements.

Seven thirty on the dot I was there, nervous and self conscious about my situation. My mum and dad were at this time waiting to be re-housed through a compulsory purchase order to widen West Derby Road. My father was up to his usual bad behaviour refusing to move or even view another property; as a consequence my family home was the last in the street. It was the most horrendous situation to be in. We were constantly being robbed, God what a nightmare. So to say I was in a highly insecure place would give you a peephole view of that nightmare scenario which I hid from my beloved Stuart.

On that first date Stu took me to the Fiddlers Ferry, a pub in Cheshire for a drink. Fiddlers Ferry was a lovely olde worlde type of pub. It was then on that first date that I noticed when the light shone on his beautiful black hair, that I could see the blue so vividly. Phenomenal! He loved the way I dressed in a tailored style with subtle shades of blue, grey and purple and green outfits. I have never had a lot of clothes in my life, but I have always been loyal to quality tailored suits and lovely accessories, just like my mother in her youth.

Fortunately, I knew he would like the Tabu cologne which smelt like toffee. Stu had always had a sweet tooth since childhood, which is typical of true to type Taureans. Sadly this was to be his downfall and tragic end. After choking on the false tooth – acquired from eating too much sugar as a little boy resulting in tooth decay – when the car landed upside down in that muddy pool, GOD, WHAT A FUCKING TRAGIC WASTE OF A UNIQUE LIFE.

His poor mother was so dignified and stoic, and carried on running their export business for ten years after Stu was killed, and then she bled to death through an allergic reaction that had gone unnoticed for years. God rest her soul. She certainly suffered after Stuart died. I know as I knew then that Mrs Howitt would have been against me having a relationship with Stu, because of the lack of wealth and materialism within my family and the constant "warring". But I'm sure that somehow down the line I would have got together with Stu Howitt. There is no question in my mind about that fact, I just know. It has been suggested to me that I was married to him in a previous life. I wanted so much to be with him for the rest of my life. But I knew the reality and facts of my life only too well!! And the restrictions it's brought me, even now!!

Stu had only one other serious relationship in his life, when he was formerly engaged to a girl called Ingrid who lived at Woolton Village and whose father was seriously wealthy. Stu informed me he broke off the two and a half year engagement because he was a "non-conformist". But he did love Ingrid; he even named his motor boat after her. He met her when he would collect his mum from Andre Bernard Hair Salon in the city centre and they started going out together. She was a hair stylist at the salon, who went to Italy to work as a nanny after the engagement was broken and subsequently married an Italian and now probably with half a dozen kids.

It was on my first date with Stu that he invited me to go up to the Lake District for a weekend with him on his boat. That's when I discovered where he had bought the boat. Yes, this was the smiling young man whom I had seen six years earlier in Boaler Street at the side of the former Cosy Cinema, buying his Motor boat, when I went cycling by. "Destiny."

You see why I pestered my Nan into giving me the card and tea-leaf readings. There was something very unusual going on, extraordinary. The reading was always the same: "A death by car accident." And it involved a Queen of Spades and King of Spades. Both Stuart's mother and father had jet-black hair, although his father's hair had gone a bit grey. Those were the cards that represented them both in this tragedy which I realized and became aware of on the day of Stuart's funeral on the 21st June 1968 at 195 Queen's Drive, Liverpool. Their next door neighbour was Brian Epstein, the Beatles' manager, who committed suicide around the same time.

Stu at Oulton Park Race Track, 1967

CHAPTER THREE
DREAM PREMONITION

I was still reeling from my first date with Stu and the invitation to the Lake District on his dad's 34ft cabin cruiser. Being a well brought up, genteel, Catholic young lady I would never at that age have been allowed to go, nor would I have had the confidence to spend a weekend on my own with such a gorgeous, sophisticated guy. I simply wouldn't leave my Nan on her own or desert my mother on our usual Saturday afternoon food shopping expeditions in town with high tea or lunch at George Henry Lees Dept Store and a drink at the Hanover Hotel and then to Reeces Luxurious food Hall in Parker Street, Clayton Square where my mother would buy her Harris sweet-cure bacon and the delicious cakes and bread that Reeces were renowned for at the time.

All my life I have been drawn to food halls, having been so lucky to have had a selection of them in Liverpool during the sixties, such as Coopers, famous for selling the best coffee beans. Which, you could smell the fantastic aroma of the those wonderful coffee beans all the way down to Queen Victoria's monument, 500 hundred feet away. My mother would take my brother and myself for ice cream and tea with knickerbockers' glory in one of the many restaurants throughout Reeces food hall. We might visit the Grill Room in the basement or the coffee shop on the ground floor of the food hall, and then over to Casey Street to a delicatessen, called, Thoroughgoods, famous for their sausages. St John's Market would be another stop for chicken and veg. My Grandmother Minnie Jackson's sister, Aunty May Waddington, had a stall selling poultry and eggs for years, as well as to the different Restaurants, in Town, they lived in Aigbuirth near the cricket ground, and we were allowed only to visit on Boxing Day when they gave a party for my dad's side of the family only. My mother wouldn't ever be invited.

In the sixties Liverpool was highly individual and diverse. Bold Street was the equivalent to Old Bond Street in London at that time. Right at the bottom of Bold Street on the right hand side used to be a boutique, Lucinda Byre, with its black and white candy stripped canopy and most unusual shop front selling the most beautiful of intercontinental fashions.

A few doors away was the family owned Cripps of Bold street, which is now Waterstones book shop with the Lyceum Club on the   left hand corner of Bold Street, Jaeger, Austin Reed, Cresta, and the most fantastic hip coffee shop selling cappuccinos which were the coolest drink in the sixties to order. England had just discovered cappuccinos in the sixties.

I was needed by my family. So I would be there. I would put my mum on the train at Exchange Street Station to Fazakerley and go home to my Nan.

I had a second date with Stuart and as usual he was waiting right outside the former cinema when I arrived. Stu was winding his watch. Another watch, I enquired? This one was a diver's watch. How many watches, do you have, I asked. A few, he answered. This time we went off to the Blundelsands Hotel for a drink where we were met by a group of his friends. I knew from the beginning that I was falling in love with him. We talked about his Haulage Business and the Lake District. Stu sensed that I didn't want to be interviewed about my life or family at that time. He wanted to get to know me first.   The diver's watch he wore that night was the one he wore the day he was killed.

I didn't hear from him for a couple of weeks, when one Saturday afternoon in town with my mum on our usual Saturday trip to town after lunch, walking down Bold Street, there was Stuart walking up towards us. He was dressed in his usual impeccable style. I was not prepared to go over and speak to him right then and there as I was having a bad hair day. I had to look my best for myself as well as for Stuart.   Fortunately he didn't see me and Mum, so we quickly followed him up the street and watched him go into Austin Reed's menswear store, halfway up Bold Street on the left hand side.

I could predict that night he would be in the Cabin Club, I just sensed it. Sure enough he came in with the pompous Wally Browne with his cut-glass accent. But I didn't buy this phoney projection for one minute, and waited no time in letting Stu know my feelings about Mr Browne. He's my general manager, he replied.

How right I was. A few years later, after Stu's death, it transpired that Browne had been stealing money from Stuart, and how the Howitts found a gun in Stu's safe with Wally

Browne's finger prints all over it. No one has seen or heard of him since after he disappeared to Norfolk. Andrew Howitt informed me of this thirty-seven years later on the 12th of December 2004 at the launch of my website of my book, "Bailey's Raw Deal". 37 was the number on the Hillman imp on that fatal day at Oulton Park, and it took thirty-seven years to meet up with the Howitts again. Joe Howitt had died a few years earlier. He lived to his early eighties, and for a few years lived in Puerto Banus in Spain.

After thirty-seven years I finally managed to obtain two black and white photographs of my beloved Stu on the launch of "Bailey's Raw Deal" website on my mum's 78th birthday.

The dream premonition that I had as a tiny child materialized on Friday the 21st June 1968 at the funeral of Stuart Howitt. Stu's death had been in the Sunday Mirror and the News of the World on Sunday the 16th of June 1968, but I did not become aware of Stu Howitt's death until Monday 17th June when a family member referred to how they had read in the Sunday papers about Stu being killed. This was told to me in a cold, matter-of-fact manner by my mother's half brother's wife June. I was so wiped out, so shocked, so devastated. I cried and cried for days!

I called the Howitts to give my condolences and to plead to be able to see Stu one last time. Olive Howitt wouldn't allow me to see her beloved favourite son in the funeral parlour. I tried a second time to no avail. Finally I gave up and went to the funeral at 195 Queen's Drive, Childwall on that sunny summer's day in the middle of June in 1968.

I arrived about an hour before the cortege arrived, taking with me a bouquet of flowers for my love. Mrs Howitt opened the front door of her huge house on Liverpool's Queen's Drive which runs right across some of the wealthiest areas of Liverpool. A slim brunette with shoulder length black hair which flicked out at the ends, dressed in a black lacy cocktail dress, dignified, composed and stoic, showing no pain as she greeted me, calling to her husband Joe to come and meet me.

As I stood on their front doorstep looking into their large marble floored hall to the right of the hallway I could see an impressive stairwell. But there was a dark shadow at over the top of the stairs, which I recall so vividly, it was so daunting, and black. A bad omen, this was the feeling and insight I felt so strongly right then and there on that front door step on this blackest of days in my piss-poor existence in Liverpool in 1968.

Joe and Olive Howitt invited me to come in and have a drink before the funeral. Alone and nervous, feeling inadequate because of my family's financial predicament, but immaculately well dressed in my purple and olive green Sybil Zelker suit with matching purple blouse and accessories, I certainly looked good. The suit which I had bought from Lucinda Byre of Bold Street, just a month before.

Joe Howitt escorted me into his bar, which was the large room on the left of the front door of this large double-fronted house full of people. I stood alone with only my vodka and lime for comfort. Jonathan, Stu's then baby brother, was running around like any nine year old would do. I tried my best to be as composed and stoic, as inconspicuous as possible, standing there in the bar of Joe Howitt's house with the small butterfly patterned tables scattered around that room.

My emotions began to get the better of me when the cortege suddenly appeared right outside the windows of 195 Queen's Drive. I do not remember who drove me to West Derby Crematorium that day. The church was full of people; there were about 130 who attended his funeral. I was invited back to the house but how I got there I have no idea. I was in a state of SHOCK and trauma. A couple more vodkas later and I was so emotional and so, so sad, with the major loss and finality at 18 years of age!

The reality was too much to deal with and take in, never to talk with Stuart again, never to be with him, this was the final, the end of an extraordinary relationship and love affair, all be it, unrequited. There is no question of my deep love for Stuart Duncan Howitt, Olive Howitt's magnificent, extremely talented, gorgeous young son. Twenty-six years of age, one month to the day into his 26th, year of life. GONE FOREVER, NO RETURN OR REPRIEVE, LOST FOR ETERNITY.

I needed to see his room one time, the only time I was ever going to be in Stu's bedroom. I wandered around the house checking with Mrs Howitt if I could be of any assistance to her. She wouldn't hear of it. I walked into the marbled hallway with the wine-coloured wall covering which Stuart had shown to me a few weeks earlier in their old house at 308 Queen's Drive from the wallpaper pattern book, and how he explained to me that everything, but everything, that could go wrong had gone wrong in the month leading up to moving to that mansion at 195 Queen's Drive. On that last time, I would be with him.

As I climbed that elegant staircase I had such a bad feeling at the top of that stairwell. In one of the bedrooms were some of Stu's relatives. One or two of his aunties were talking to a small group of females as I walked in, crying quietly, something was said in relation to the tragedy and great loss and I was quickly put in my place by his aunt, that they had known Stuart all his life and really only they had the right to feel their great loss and sadness. This was an extremely cruel statement on that day of blackness and pain in my young life, I was a very sensitive and caring young girl. How could they not accept how I felt and what I had lost, how much he meant to me in my hard, difficult life?

Not wanting to get into any argument or to offend anyone I walked into the landing at the side of the elegant staircase. I stopped right in the middle of that landing staring at the red mock flock wallpaper and just crying quietly when I began to wonder which one of the bedrooms was Stu's, when right then the door to my right, which was not properly closed, started to glide slowly open at that precise time I was asking myself about his bedroom, which room could it be, and I heard a whisper, an inner voice repeatedly telling me to go into the room.

I paused, worrying if Stu's relatives were to find me in Stuart's bedroom they might chuck me out. Whilst I was repeatedly being given the instruction, go in the room, I noticed from the landing that in the small window recess stood Stu's driving trophies, so it was confirmed that this was the bedroom! I looked back at the stairwell, staring at that wallpapered wall, when in a flash I was transported back to the dream I had when I was four years of age living with my beloved Nan at 42 Lavan Street. "The Dream" I was so afraid of even thinking about, let alone to be able to discuss it with anyone. This was the place, this was the day, this was why I was so petrified when the dream came back to me, weeks after dreaming of this place the black shadow cast over the top of that albeit elegant stairwell at 195 Queen's Drive.

On this day of days in the extraordinary life of Patricia Jackson, Jackson being my maiden name, I was literally mentally and emotionally transported back in time to that "Dream Premonition" all those years earlier. I have barely come to terms with this highly charged awareness of this all-important day in my lifespan then and now some 38 years later.

When the friends and relatives walked out into Stuart's bedroom I quickly followed them in, where there was a small selection of black and white photographs of Stuart. These were meant for me, albeit some thirty-seven years later I got to own two of these same photos plus a racing car trophy from October 67 at Aintree Race Track. Andrew Howitt finally gave in to my pleading for a picture of Stu. To be fair it's just a tad unusual to receive a call from your dead brother's girlfriend some thirty-seven years later. Oh boy, did Andrew Howitt grill me with questions during two hours of telephone conversations. Eventually I gave too many precise dates and details for me to be unreal or a sick joker, as he originally thought I could be.

Andrew and Jonathan and their wives and children couldn't resist my invitation to my launch at the Radisson Hotel in Liverpool, a New Moon that Sunday the, 12th December 2004. Having been born on a New Noon it is particularly important to begin any new venture or business idea on a New Moon for anyone, according to ancient beliefs. But especially so if you are born on a New Moon, it's absolutely essential. God only knows I try my best to augur good fortune in my direction, which somehow seems to escape me.

Andrew has since informed me that his mother discovered what was behind the white marbled fireplace in the hall. It was later revealed to them that the builders they employed to renovate 195 Queen's Drive had bought and used grave-stones to place at the back of those beautiful marbled fireplaces. This was really a bad omen. The fireplace was directly below the landing where I stood on that blackest of days in my life on the 21st June 1968 after the funeral of Stuart Duncan Howitt when I was awakened to my "Dream

Premonition" of 13 years earlier. It is so uncanny!!! So unbelievable, so real, so true!

CHAPTER FOUR
PHOTOGRAPHS

Every day since I obtained the old black and white sepia photographs of my beloved Stu after waiting thirty-seven years for a picture of him, there hasn't been a day that I don't touch or kiss and talk to Stu Howitt's pictures. How different my life could have been with this sensuous of Taureans, gentle and so tender-loving, I have long realized there was only one reason there could be in this gentle of gentlemen meeting me all those years ago, and that the conclusion has to be for me to have the great privilege to write about his "greatness" and "uniqueness", albeit 38 years later. And what better day to start this story, it had to be on his birthday May 15th 2006 on what would have been his 64th year. I have had the notion of writing a book about Stu and the Dream Premonition since the late seventies.

In one of the two photographs there are a group of four guys, Stuart included, having a drink in Palma de Mallorca Bar. They had obviously taken his dad's boat for the trip, with St Tropez being his favourite port of call. He would be only about twenty-one in the picture, the spitting image of his mother at that time. The second picture is of another group, a foursome with Ingrid and I believe Wally Browne and a girl. Curiously about a year or so before I came into owning these treasured photographs, I dreamt of a darkened large room, similar to a theatre, with an audience as a huge play was being acted out with spotlights shining onto a group of four silhouettes in the darkness with a mirror background with the spotlight bouncing off the mirror. This is the picture in my dream which took some months before I recalled this scene in the dream.

Over the years this has happened quite a few times hitherto in my life but never as profoundly or fearsome as the first Dream Premonition at the funeral of Stu Howitt. It's more or less a snapshot of a place, a street, a house which is photographed and stored in my mind's eye until the day arrives to frequent or visit albeit briefly it may be for me to remember the photographic dream.

There's no question that my first recollection of my Dream Premonition has been the most prolific of all. Simply another form of clairvoyance. My destiny! It took thirteen and a half years to materialize. This is my cross which I will carry for the rest of my life, according to many psychics that I have come across, especially in the past few years, Robin Lund, International Palmist, was no exception. Robin pointed out, the Cross in both of my hands, after inquiring what happened to you at 18 years of age? Last August the after my birthday, on the 25th of August 06.

Less than a year after meeting Andrew and Jonathan Howitt and their children Jonathan naturally named his first son after his older brother so there is another Stu Howitt on the planet, although he looked nothing like his late uncle Stuart but was as mannerly and charming as Uncle Stuart , but the resemblance is quite striking between Andrew and Stu, and sometimes during my telephone interrogations he sounded just like Stu Howitt, incredibly so that for a moment I felt I was talking to Stuart, uncanny.

For many months after receiving the beautiful old photographs, I was haunted every day by my darling Stuart, it encapsulated me each and every day, the haunting grew stronger and stronger, totally, and then things in my apartment with my partying, self obsessed neighbour reached a peak and I decided to call a psychic medium that I had seen advertised in the Evening Standard to detoxify any negativity or bad vibes in my flat or that may have been surrounding me.

I wasn't sure as to whether or not I should have this person visit me alone in my flat, but things were reaching a boiling point with legal issues relating to the false accusations from my egotistical neighbour, and I urgently needed some help in dealing with anti social situation. This was November 2005. I rang the psychic to cancel our appointment, but during my call to the psychic he insisted on keeping his appointment with me. He informed me how he believed that he strongly felt as though I had been stabbed in the heart in previous lives and that he felt that this was the case in this lifespan as well.

There is not a lot you can say after that statement, except to agree to the appointment. I needed all the understanding and help I could get to deal with this negative nuisance, two year problematic situation getting any further out of hand so I could sell at the market value of the flat and move away from this problematic immature egotist.

I decided that I would go down to the ground floor and meet the psychic at the front door of the building to give me a chance to decide if I got the right vibe from him. The psychic arrived, looking every inch like a vicar in every sense of the word: actions, speech, demeanor and appearance, slim and slightly greying hair with a moustache, dressed in clerical grey. Still not entirely convinced I asked whether we should go in the north side entrance of the building, in order for me to check him out further. The psychic spoke to his spirit guides on different levels, before deciding that this was the way to enter.

We quickly arrived up to the fifth floor to my apartment, flat 3. The moment he stepped over the front door he gasped. I checked with him whether it was a negative or a positive gasp. He replied that it was an exclamation of how lovely my flat looked. But, the bad news being he was convinced that I was "CURSED. Now, and in previous lives." He then told me it would take a couple of hours to detoxify the negativity away from me from any previous and for any further lives, and from this moment in time.

Outside of my family no one had seen my treasured black and white old photographs of Stu so as a little test I showed the mirrored picture with Ingrid and Stu, the foursome group, to see if he would tell me which man was Stuart. He chose the right guy. Throughout this ritual I was asked if I wanted to be connected to Stu Howitt for all time. Yes, I replied without any hesitation. It was put to Stu: could I write this story about him? Yes, came the reply, and that allegedly I had been married to Stu in a previous life.

At the end of the detox I was assured that all curses and negativity were cut away from me for eternity and to visualize a heart shape on the wall which joined the flat next door to my flat, and to colour the heart shape with the colour pink to send love towards him, to erase the poisonous venom from Flat 4 projected at me.

For many weeks the exhaustion persisted which everyone commented on. I called the medium, which did not care for my honest comments, he didn't want to hear the reality that things had got worse with the owner of Flat 4 and how I felt was just so dreadful. He then got very angry and excited with me and asked did I want my £40 returned. No, I stated, just an explanation or reason for the situation which had become extreme now since the detox of "curses" and negativity. A few days went by and the returned cheque for £40 arrived in the post.

So it did not work for me. But no one could accuse me of not trying to progress and move forward. It would seem to be the way it goes for me. Oh how good it must be to have good neighbours and able to get on with your life without so many trials and tribulations. Just because you live in a place to have to deal with these unnecessary hurdles and problems every day which in turn devalues the market value on the property, this being the only means I have left open to me since the sudden and unexpected death of my late husband, Peter Bailey.

The Bailey left me destitute after paying off all of his debts of over £50,000 fifteen years ago. I have reinvented myself a few times since then because I had no option, other than to survive or sink. No one offered me a job so I made my own with property speculation, which has been an ongoing nightmare with all manner of problematic situations to deal with whilst trying to sell and move on to the next. This was the only way I've had of making any money to survive if I was going to continue living in London.

CHAPTER FIVE
NEW YEAR'S EVE

December 1977 New Year's Eve, the second Christmas that I had been married to Peter Bailey whom I had met at the Five Star Oriel Restaurant in Water Street, Liverpool on the 7th March 1975, just three and a half months after losing my highly philanthropic, magnanimous Nan.

My Grandmother played so many vital roles in my extremely difficult, impecunious life. At that time in Liverpool there was no availability to live on credit cards or easy access to loans or property speculation. People largely survived on what little they had, and families helped one another. There were few jobs available in Liverpool in the sixties and early seventies, and the applicants outweighed the positions every time except for the family-run businesses and the Jewish communities. Footballers and pop stars, and of course the legal firms and courts were always busy as usual, with the illegal pursuits which generally run parallel with poverty and lack of opportunity in cities across the world. But that's how people survived in Liverpool back then, and I don't believe that times have changed that much really in Liverpool or elsewhere in England in 2006. People live mainly on credit cards and loans.

The grossly oversold and overrated award of European city of Culture 2008 was won by Liverpool a few years ago. Unfortunately with a little research on former European cities that won this same award, Stockholm, Cork, Glasgow, nothing much happens after the first few weeks hyper hype ballooning which tends to be paramount in today's world, which people should be advised of, together with any bonuses of such an award. Great expectations!!

On the 17th July 1976 I married Peter Bailey, eight years after Stu was killed and eighteen months after my Nan died. My marriage to Bailey had already become violent and cruel. When my Nan died I had all this love and tenderness to give, with no one to give it to. Then PB arrived with his quiet, charming manner, serious and clever, well travelled and popular, athletic, knowledgeable but set in his chauvinistic ways, a man's man by his own admission, with a large capacity to indulge in booze and good food too frequently on a daily basis. With no interest to think ahead, no stability, no security, live now and someone would have to pay later, there was never any security put by for me should anything happen to him, and this possibility was high because of the drinking and the age difference. This confirmed married bachelor, as I became more and more conscious of over the eighteen and a half years I was with him, never wanted me to gain from the marriage in any way. Which took ten years of bereavement to realize it totally; he purposefully left me high and dry. There is no question in my mind of that fact. I paid everyone Bailey owed of the £50,000 or so that was owed on his death without exception.

But on this New Year's in December 1977 I had hope and love and belief that we would make a lovely home together and perhaps open a small bistro within the first five years of marriage which Bailey kidded me along into believing for a few years of that marriage, before declaring that he would never do anything other than marine consultancy, ever.

New Year's Eve 1977 we booked a table at the Oriel Restaurant where we were first introduced by a family friend, Joseph Kelly, a former Mayor of Bootle, a suburb in Liverpool. Kelly introduced Peter Bailey to my mother and me on the 7th March 1975. It was a Friday evening and my mum and I were still grieving our great loss of my Grandmother, my mother's mother Sarah Middleton Joyce, when Kelly came into the Oriel with Peter Bailey.

Before New Year's Eve of 1977 I had been physically abused quite badly by Peter the first Easter of that marriage in April 1977. Nine years had already passed since Stu's fatality in June 1968. I had spoken to Olive Howitt only once when I bumped into her in Henderson Department Store a few months after the funeral and chased after her to give her my sympathy and condolences. Mrs Howitt did not ask me to visit her; she seemed reluctant to talk about her bereavement, only to enquire about what I did for a living, nothing more than that, just small talk before she disappeared into the crowds of Church Street.

I saw her only once again (coming out the back entrance of Reeces Food Hall) until New Years Eve 1977, in the Oriel Restaurant. How incredible is this to have Olive and Joe Howitt sitting on the next table to Bailey and myself. Joe Howitt seemed relaxed, jovial and showing no pain. On the table was the usual party stuff for New Year's Eve. But I noticed Joe Howitt wearing a party mask which was of a skull. Olive was as composed and dignified as ever as I remembered from the funeral. But I could still feel her pain as I sat alongside of her and Joe Howitt. I did not want to upset her by introducing myself; it was not the right time or place. Not that she needed any reminding of her great loss from me. I decided to let it rest for her sake.

Olive Howitt died some seven years later on 2nd April 1985. She bled to death before the ambulance got to the hospital, having collapsed with a perforated ulcer. Olive Howitt I know never recovered from Stu's fatality. She simply died of a "broken heart". God rest her soul. When I recall that New Year's Eve in Liverpool 1977 I believe I made the right decision, although I really wanted to talk to them both. But, how could I. Joe Howitt lived to be 85 years of age. He lived in Spain on his boat for a few years before developing Alzheimer's a few years before I gave my book launch in Liverpool, and meeting up again with Stu's brothers and their families on Sunday 12th December 2004.

Olive worked for their import and export business, employing and running over a hundred staff. Olive ran their family business for over ten years. The Howitts continued to live at 195 Queen's Drive for many years after the tragic accident of Stu Howitt, before moving over the water on the Wirral peninsula from Liverpool. It is obvious that there was some significance in that final meeting between Olive and Joe Howitt on New Years Eve 1977, and "The Bailey" and myself, no question. I was meant to see and identify and above all to recall and remember the "Great Love of my Life" and what might have been, if only –

And perhaps it was an all powerful message from Stuart to know that we should have been together with his family for that New Year's Eve, because in a way I was sharing that New Year with Stu's family and Stuart, even though Olive and Joe were unaware of it.

Jonathan, the youngest son of the Howitt family, tells me they never talked about Stuart after he was killed. Olive and Joe decided that it was too unbearably painful to talk about, so they chose not to discuss their great loss and tragedy. This is so wrong!!!

Having had a lot of bereavement in my life, I long since realized it is absolutely essential to shed the grief and pain and in order to keep that person's spirit alive you simply must talk about them. It takes a good ten years to work your way through the grieving process. You cannot paint someone out of the family picture because of their passing, as any bereavement consultant or psychotherapist would agree.

I now realize I am the messenger to the Howitt brothers on behalf of the Love of my Life, Stuart. That he feels left out and saddened naturally, because of their reluctance to talk about him. He needs them to recognise him as their older brother who loved them and took them out on trips as he did with his beloved mother Olive. HE CARED ABOUT THEM VERY MUCH. It's my destiny to give them this message, albeit thirty-nine years later (March 2007). Up to this point in time I was totally unaware of the fact that they were not able to discuss Stu Howitt's passing.

CHAPTER SIX
SEDUCTION

Saturday 10th February 1968 has been one of the rarest of magic days in my life, unforgettable, if not the rarest hitherto, thirty eight years later I am still consumed by that magic of nights that fate gave to us, indescribable, utterly sensuous, tender, pure, gentle and oh so real. It was TRUE LOVE IN ALL ITS GLORY.

How else could those beautiful rare feelings stay so fresh and have such impact within me, all these years later? How can anyone explain the Dream and Prediction, and our subsequent brief meetings over the thirteen years before I got to meet the "Love of my Life" and even since the tragedy of Stuart and on New Year's Eve 1977. Why did I get to sit next to Olive Howitt on New Year's Eve?

Joe Howitt died broke, but able to live for a few years on his boat in Puerto Banus in sunny Spain appearing to have it all, an enjoyable lifestyle. The resemblance between Andrew and Stu is quite uncanny. The upright stance, shoulders back posture, the build, the height, eyes and sometimes Andrew's voice sounds so much like Stu's. God oh God! Two years ago when I had a series of telephone calls with Andrew it sounded and felt as thought it was Stu Howitt calling me. It really blew me away. Wow!

Jonathan when I looked more closely bore a great intense look in his eyes like his late brother, and his expressions and great charm and manners. Mr and Mrs Howitt did an excellent job on the upbringing of their sons. For sure that cannot be denied. I am sure they were both so proud of their sons.

It must have been a couple of weeks before the fatal accident at Oulton Park, the last time I ever saw Stu Howitt. On that Saturday in May 1968 I had seen him in Bold Street with my mother Lillian when we followed Stu up Bold Street when I wasn't looking my best to be able to go and speak to him on that Saturday afternoon. But I was given another chance, thank God, to see him later that same day in the Cabin Club. This was the night Stu took me back to their old house at 308 Queen's Drive in his white Ford Mustang with dark red leather seats and left-hand drive. The seat was a complete seat that was in one piece inside the car, door to door.

We were greeted by his boxer dog "Sooner" in the hallway of his mother's large ex-council semi-detached house, the opposite end of Queen's Drive in Walton to their new home at 195 Queen's Drive. Queen's Drive runs about nine or ten miles across Liverpool. Packing boxes stood on the hallway. There were books of materials and wall coverings. Stu even showed me the wallpaper that was chosen for the elegant stairwell, although on that night I had no recollection of the wine-coloured wallpaper with the mock flock design which was the vogue at that time. This didn't register until the day of the funeral on Friday 21st June 1968 when the premonition came home to roost. After many years of New Moons had passed in my lifespan, that all fearful foreboding dream that haunted me as a tiny child for weeks, too afraid to speak of it to anyone let alone recall it. The intensity of the fear that returned with each flashback each and every time it returned was indescribable, especially for such a stoic, highly sensitive little creature like me. It's just to uncanny for words. This was my fate, predestined premonition, to prepare me for my waiting destiny at that house in Queen's Drive on 21st June 1968.

God alone knows how much Stu Howitt meant to me. I'm sure Olive Howitt sensed the depth of my feelings at first glance on her doorstep on that Friday in June 1968. A few months before, strange as it was, I had been suffering really black moods and feelings of great despair. I had made a mental note of it and referred it to my Grandmother. It always manifested on Fridays with such a force and would peter out over the weekends during the run-up to the fatality on that Saturday in June 1968.

The despair of blackness stopped and never returned after that Friday 21st June 1968. Never again from that funeral Friday did that blackness return. It was preparation for the great tragedy in my life that was about to happen, as was the Dream Premonition all those years earlier.

We feasted on tender affection and sensuality once more on that last meeting in Olive Howitt's house, the extent of our emotions were so strong, my darling Stu didn't realize he had put on his new shoes that he had bought earlier that day on the wrong feet until we got into his dad's Jaguar, to drive me home. It was then I had to ask the question if he valued things. What I was really asking him was, if I were to lose my virginity to him would he value me and my love for him, or would he take me for granted. Stu responded that he was a non-conformist.

On the way home to my Nan's apartment, just as we were approaching Sheil Road from Rocky Lane, Stu told me that he was "so very fond" of me and how very pretty he found me. I was still on my guard, afraid to believe him in case it was just a line. I answered in a repellant response telling him not to be stupid, this is how little awareness and confidence that I held of my attractiveness at the time. Highly critical! He then told me he didn't care too much being called stupid. Quite right too! How the hell did I manage to say such a ridiculous comment to the man I loved so affectionately and deeply?

I rang Stuart once more, and much to my great surprise he answered the phone. I remember I had my transistor playing in the background, Tom Jones was singing Delilah, as Stu in his most gentle of voices repeatedly said hello! I was certain he had a notion it was probably me calling him. I never spoke and placed the receiver down and ran down the hall to my Nan to tell her Stu had answered the phone. For a few minutes I really thought about phoning back but lost my nerve. That was the last communication with that gentle of gentlemen, Stu Howitt. A couple of weeks later all was lost forever. No more phone calls, no dates, no Cabin Club. Finito! For Stuart and I, no reprieve.

It would have been just a matter of weeks before the depth of my emotions got the better of me and I would surrender to the "Great Love of my Life". It was just a matter of time. We both knew and realized the force of our emotions right from the start. There was just something so indefinable about our relationship. Each and every time I find myself in Rocky Lane or Boaler Street the memories flood back to me in such vivid detail and texture. The words he spoke, his declaration of his feelings for me have never left me nor do I expect they ever will. His gentleness, the soft spoken tender way he always spoke to me, Jesus, why did you let this happen to him and me?

People in the Cabin Club were always trying to warn me to be careful with Stu. I suspected they were envious of him. How he would tell of the women he knew in St Tropez and how he loved blondes. They were trying to protect me.

I took notice and did my best to protect myself and not have to regret doing anything too soon or too risky. How different I am sure I would have been if I had realized that the card readings were about Stuart. I certainly wouldn't have taken so long in calling him in the hopeful expectation of being able to see him more if he would have let me. And definitely I would have gone on his boat to the lakes. How euphorically romantic would that have been. The thing is how you would get over that, I'm still in recovery. You never get over bereavement but simply learn to live with it. This is so true.

CHAPTER SEVEN
SPECULATION

Looking back, having travelled down the road of my life, knowing what lay in store throughout the ensuing years with Bailey and Peter Engen. Through all the violence and abuse, destitution and litigation, being alone without any real prospects except when I married a second time which was very short-lived in the great expectation department. Reality came bulldozing in once again. So you just get on with the hand the life has dealt you, that's all you can do apart from hope and pray and do your best and make the most of what you have and be grateful for what little you have. "Life's a bastard and then you die!!" and who knows of what is beyond the grave, if anything. No one ever came back to tell the tale. Not yet.

Bailey was always amazed at how I would refer to life and death awareness. But the aftermath of his sudden death made me more aware of how little time we have on the planet and to totally abhor time-wasters and time lost, throughout the past fifteen years since Bailey died. Bailey was such a fool, his deep rooted insecurity and chauvinism was his ruination.

He lived for the moment, believing he would live forever so long as he ate well and exercised and kept his brain alert with being interested in anything and everything. During those sixteen and a half years he would tell me how I was the biggest sobering effect in his entire life. He would assure me that I would always have him. Wrong again, Bailey. My marriage meant so much to me so I stuck with it and gave the best to PB and the marriage. Unfortunately I now realize that he didn't want to accept responsibility or do right by me. He refused to accept that dying is a part of life. He couldn't bear to even think about it. So there was no chance of discussing it, what I would do if he were to die.

For the first few years after "Our Cathedral Wedding" in Liverpool Metropolitan Cathedral of Christ the King. He would leave me to go on some concocted trips to Iceland, Ireland, Hull, anywhere he could to try and get me to leave him and subsequently divorce him, that was one of his scams to get out of the marriage. But I had gone through too much in life as well as with Bailey and his former women friends. I intended to make the marriage work, at least I tried but he made it extremely difficult for me and me and my impecunious, close-knit family.

In those days I had a lot of entertaining to do because of his job which I did reluctantly after always being treated like a second class citizen and being constantly reminded of how lucky I was to have married the great Peter Bailey, and who he could have married. Then there were the deceptions and secrets which I sensed after the first few months. Up to that point in time I was so in love with him and happy that we would have a chance of building a nice home together. Bailey changed the minute we got married and would portray me in a bad light to one and all, this was how insecure he was which stemmed from his childhood in Tynemouth and living through the wartime as an evacuee. Leaving home at twenty-one for the Merchant Navy and becoming a Chief Engineer at twenty-six years which was quite an accomplishment at such a young age.

I don't believe that I ever felt the same towards the marriage after the first time he hit me, Easter 1977. He was cruel and mean to me through that sixteen and a half years of a so-called marriage. I cannot help but remember the man, the Love of my Life Stu Howitt, if only things had gone the way they should. If only Stu wouldn't have been killed there was hope that someday we would have met up. I know his mother had wanted the world for him but no one would have loved him more than me, ever.

Stu told me once that he was a non-conformist. Little did he know that I was too, only much more than him for sure. I never wanted the semi-detached with a couple of kids which totally consumes one's life. It wasn't what I ever wanted and I never got it either. Nor did I ever intend to live my whole life in Liverpool. I just knew at seventeen that I would not be there for all my life, even before I met Stuart Howitt or Peter Bailey. Stu and I had so much in common, which I have come to realize over the past thirty-nine years.

If I were to have got pregnant with Stu's baby I wouldn't have held him to ransom. I could not put my family through that pain and anguish. My father would have gone ballistic, my wonderful Nan would have been blamed, and I would not have ever lived it down with my mother or my brother, as well as being despised by Mrs Howitt. I could not have coped with it all. Stu had the world at his feet and I had no intention to mess that up. I didn't want him to hate me. If we would have got together it was going to be him coming back for me, nothing less would do. I know I would have made him happy and he had the most calming effect on me and such a long lasting impact through all the years since 1968. If anybody was so right for me it was him!! He was exactly what I always wanted.

Having found someone so unique, so rare and then to have him snatched away forever is just too sad and unjust to bear thinking about, let alone to live with. But that's how it was. The memories will haunt me forever, at least I have those and the photographs to hold on to, along with one of his prize trophies for racing. It has taken me such a long time to getting around to writing this story which I have talked about and promised to write since the beginning of the eighties. I located the Howitts who were then living on the Wirral and spoke to the sisters-in-law of Stuart and informed them of my intentions of writing my story on their late brother in law. But it was not till 2004 that I actually met them again since 1968. It could only have been the reason for me to have known Stu Howitt for me to be able to write this "Sad Love Story" about the brief time we had together and how hugely extraordinarily talented he was with luck galore in everything he turned his hand to, except for that fatal day at Oulton Park Race Track. That is the only thing wrong with luck, when it starts to run out it runs faster than quicksilver and never returns. This can be the only reason I believe for my date with destiny. "To write about him."

And secondly and perhaps more importantly, I now realize in view of the fact that the Howitt family never spoke about Stuart I know now that there is a message I had to bring to Stuart's family, keep his spirit alive, TALK ABOUT HIM. Hopefully, my story will enhance the life and memory of Stuart Duncan Howitt. Immortalize him that is my desire and great privilege to try and do this for him.

CHAPTER EIGHT
JOE'S BAR-ROOM

Since the age of three my passion for the greatest
steeplechase on the planet, Liverpool's own Grand National,
grew stronger with the passing of years in my lifespan. I
recall the first magical outing with my Great Aunt Mary, the
younger half-sister of my maternal Grandmother, Sarah.
The Grand National is quite reminiscent of my life in a great
many respects. Strangely enough the first time I picked the
winner of the National was in 1968 when Red Alligator
won. This was to be the first of my many winners of the
world's greatest steeplechase. Just a couple of months
before Stu's untimely tragic accident, stranger still on the
reunion at my website launch Andrew Howitt brought me
one of the many trophies from his brother's racing
achievements, from 10th October 1965 at Aintree, which was
used for many years as a car-racing track, besides National
Hunt horse-racing.

It was a few days after the 2005 Grand National
whilst I was in Liverpool and had gone up for the race, with
the reunion after thirty-seven years still fresh in my mind's
eye from meeting the Howitt brothers again, that I decided
to re-visit the Howitt's former family home at 195 Queen's
Drive, Childwall. I had taken my mother out to lunch and
suddenly I found myself right outside that house.
I quickly drove into the large driveway, leaving my mother
and Peter Engen in the car. Fortunately the electronic gates
were open, so I was able to walk up to the front door. The
same front door that I stood at all those thirty-seven years
earlier on that funeral Friday 21st June 1968. As I stood
there I could see through the glass front door that elegant
stairwell and marble fireplace in the hallway to the left of
the staircase. The marble floor looked as new as it did all
those years ago.
I knocked a second time; I just had to see inside this house
once more. No sign of life, no one home, as I started to
walk away I realized that the windows were long and low. I
walked back to the left side window of that double-fronted
house of 195 Queen's Drive. I couldn't believe my eyes.
Joe Howitt's Bar-room was still intact all those thirty-seven
years later. Still standing at the bar were the three bar

stools, and scattered around the bar room, albeit faded, were the small round butterfly tables that were brand new on that blackest of days in my lifespan back in June 1968. It was as thought this house was frozen in time ready and waiting for my re-visit. It's just incredible. I just couldn't believe my eyes.

I realized I was being watched by the next door neighbour, a Jewish lady who had brought the house from Brian Epstein. I asked her about the new owner of 195. Oh, you have just missed him, she said in reply to my enquiry. I needed to know how long the owner had lived there. It turned out that he was the one who bought the house from Olive and Joe Howitt in 1978, a builder, and it was unusual that he had kept the house in the same design for all that time especially being in the building trade. But I know only too well that there is something extraordinary about 195 Queen's Drive. I knew that then, as I do now. I then drove down to 308 Queens Drive just to have one more look, down the memory lane of my life .The next day in Liverpool, I had to visit, the Cabin Club, in Wood street, right behind Bold street, walking up, Seel Street,which I had done so many times before, each step I took on those Cobblestones. It felt just as though I was going to my job ,at the Cabin Club, just like it did all those years ago, when I was Eighteen. Extraordinary, but so real! It was early afternoon, Peter Engen was insisting that I shouldn't on knock on the door of the Cabin, but I needed to see inside the Club just one more time. Peter kept repeating that no one would be in the Club at that time, of the day. But I was determined. Once again I found myself knocking on the door were my waiting Destiny, had awaited for me , nearly, Forty years ago. I rang the bell a second time, no reply Third time lucky, I heard someone running up the stairs, behind the door, then, suddenly, the door flung open wide. Two men stood on the stairwell, I could hear myself saying I'm the Cook from the Cabin, come in one of the men replied, this was Clive the son of the Owner Brian, who gave me the job all those years ago, Clive looked nothing like his dad, Brian was now suffering from Alzheimer's, Clive explained to me, with an update on the former staff, of the Cabin. Only two days earlier, had the refurbishment began, on my Kitchen Incredible. Clive was a real good guy, so friendly and real. I reminisced about the night I met Stu Howitt right there in the Bistro were we stood it was just as it was, all those years earlier, pure Magic. As any one whom new the Cabin would agree. It was a Phenomenal Place!

My mother Lillian was not too keen on me visiting 195 Queens Drive, ever again. I felt even more aware than ever of the "Dream Premonition" as a tiny child, and the subsequent tragedies within the Howitt family. I remember on that Sunday night, 12th December 2004, Andrew arrived first with his wife, jean, a slim lady who seemed somewhat frustrated about something in her life. Jonathan and Helen and his two young sons arrived from St Nick's church in Water Street at Liverpool's Pier Head. Looking at them sitting in this small lounge at the Radisson Hotel, there was an aura which I can only describe as blackness, sadness, which I believed was relating to Olive Howitt's sudden death and Stu's fatality. But, I was wrong. There was even more tragedy waiting to happen. Joe Howitt lived for many years after he lost his beloved wife Olive. He died at 85 years of Alzheimer's in hospital in Cheshire. A few years, after Olive's sudden death Joe found a new companion. Unfortunately because of his illness the relationship was doomed. The Howitts enjoyed their cruising winter sun six week breaks throughout their married life, so it was no surprise to his sons that he should continue to cruise with his new companion, albeit short lived. Joe died on the 6th June 1998.

For many years Joe was quite friendly with my great-uncle on my father's side, Sidney Foyne. Like Joe he was a Freemason and factory owner in ship repair in Liverpool during the sixties. As I have stated many times, the "warring family" of mine would not have spoken the truth or facts about my beloved Magnanimous Nan, Sarah, which again would have had some impact on our future relationship. Siddy would have blacklisted my Grandmother to Joe Howitt. This was the unforgivable maliciousness of my father .... and scandal to his mother during his weekly visits to seek sympathy and financial assistance from his poor mother, Minnie, who adored her only son as she did her husband John whom she always referred to as her Prince on a white horseback.

My Grandfather could and should have treated this lady so much more genteelly and kindly. She was a gem of a wife and mother. Such a hard worker who ran a successful greengrocer business for well over fifteen years doing all the hard manual work that my Granddad and father should have done, as well as being an excellent cook and seamstress, laundress and loving mother. My Granddad gave my Grandmother a real "hard life". She was so loving and practical, so respectable, all she had to look forward to was to visit my great Aunt Lilly at her mini market shop on the corner of Boaler Street and catch up with the family gossip with her sisters May, Claire and Doris, the baby of the Foyne family, who would become her brother Siddy's housekeeper at 55 Buttermere Road, Huyton, for many years until he got involved with his P.A., Hilda. I loved that house which my Aunty Doris looked after with such tender loving care. A large detached house, built to my Uncle Sid's specifications. Complete with a Gym.

My Aunty May ran a successful market stall for years in St John's Market in Parker Street in Liverpool's Town Centre supplying restaurants with eggs and poultry. She lived in Allerton with the affluent Jewish community. My Aunty Claire was very placid and calm. There were also two brothers, Jackie and Sidney – seven children in all. My uncle Sid died at fifty-two with a massive heart attack in his gym at 55 Buttermere Road, in 1969, leaving the house and business to his fiancée Hilda. So my Aunty Doris, a spinster, was left homeless and destitute. Had it not been for her sister, my Aunty Lilly, taking her in and giving her a roof over her head above her general shop where I had worked as a child, I don't know what Doris would have done. It was very unjust.

It was at this time just shortly before his sudden death that my Grandfather, John Jackson, had a heart attack. My Granddad became a postman/driver for the Royal Mail for thirty-five years and after retirement he would work two nights a week for the Post Office sorting mail which we believe brought on the heart attack. My Uncle Sid was driving his sister Minnie back and forth to Walton Hospital on a daily basis. This was such a benefit to my hardworking

Grandmother Minnie who was of quite highly strung nervous disposition because of the cruel treatment from my Granddad. She was so pleased and proud that her brother Siddy was helping her at her hour of need. Then, bang, my uncle Sid dies. My poor Grandma had the awful task of having to tell my Granddad, who was enjoying the daily banter with his brother-in-law Siddy. This naturally enough had an enormous impact on my Granddad's well-being, but he lived on to outlive my Grandmother. Siddy Foyne was a great pal and business associate of Joe Howitt.

CHAPTER NINE
HIT AND RUN

The summer of 2006 on another visit back home I read a
headline: "Hit and Run Drunk Driver". In Moreton on June
10th a woman was killed by a drunk driver. The headline
gave no name as I recall. I never got to finish the article in
the Liverpool Echo. It wasn't until towards the end of
October 2006 when I had reached Chapter Five referring to
Olive Howitt on New Year's Eve 1977, that I needed to
check with Andrew on a couple of details about his late
mother. I had tried many times during the summer and
autumn to reach him but no response. Then on this sunny
October morning I rang him on his mobile and got through.
Andrew had been trying to find my number but he had lost
his computer. He wanted to tell me that Jean had been
killed.

They had just returned from Spain which is their main
residence. Jean was recovering from a broken foot. The
foot accident happened in Spain. She was advised to walk
to improve the broken foot only a day earlier back in
Moreton on the Wirral, it was on virtually her first walk
right outside the apartment in Leasowe village, a former
hospital converted in to flats that the next Howitt tragedy
was waiting to "happen". Jean was only fifty-one years of
age, with everything to look forward to with their new life in
Spain in a house built to their specification, albeit the
property took double the time to be built and with things
going wrong all the time it took nearly two years to move
into. I reminded Andrew of the difficulties they had before
their move to 195, Queens Drive , and how this might not be
the thing to do. It was too much of a parallel and maybe, he
should reconsider the move to Spain. Andrew had also
undertaken a large new business property venture in Costa
Del Caldi with a business partner, having had his former
factory burn down whilst being burgled without any
insurance. This he told me haunts him still.

As if these things weren't bad enough when you start
to believe it's got to get better. Six months after the fatal
accident of his wife Jean, Andrew has been diagnosed with
cancer of the mouth, having to have his teeth removed and
some of his tongue to remove the tumor from his jaw at

Liverpools Walton Hospital next week, March 2007. His doctors tell him that it is because of stress and smoking, which he did to quash the distress of losing his business. All those years earlier. Unable to continue to work or eat solid food since Christmas 2006, he now sits in the flat alone with the reminder and visualization of his late wife's tragic accident right outside his window, every day. Fortunately his only child Davina, 23 years old, is the only comfort he now has. Davina I am told bears a strong resemblance to her late Granddad Joe in personality. An extrovert! Thank God Andrew has his Daughter, to care for him. What she must be going through having just lost her poor Mum to some lunatic drunk driver who got six years for mowing Jean Howitt down. Andrew explains how lucky he was to have escaped within inches of his life that cruelly took the life of his wife Jean, and then this. Tomorrow is promised to no one.

It will be many months for Andrew to have some resemblance of a recovery. Andrew is as dignified and stoic as his mother. I am sure that Jonathan and Helen will be there for Andrew. Jonathan shows the traits of a down to earth Virgo, precise, hardworking, responsible, caring and humane, loyal and suspicious. I should know having researched the subject since the age of thirteen, and being a true to type Virgoan myself.

CHAPTER TEN
BOOK SIGNING

On March 1st 2007, "World Book Day", I had a book-signing for my book, *Bailey's Raw Deal* at Waterstone's in Bold Street, Liverpool, at 1.00 pm. Jonathan Howitt was in Liverpool on jury service that week and decided to pop along to my singing. Andrew was in hospital getting ready for major surgery in Aintree Hospital, obviously unable to make it. Jonathan, the baby of the Howitt brothers, was nine when his brother was killed at Oulton Park Race Track in 1968 so it would have been difficult for him to remember or know very much about Stuart, but out of curiosity and good manners I felt before closing this "Chapter in my life" I wanted some contribution from him and anyone and everyone who knew Stuart in his childhood and his life.

Jonathan referred me to their cousin John Tierl who was his Mothers sisters' son, the same age as Stu and he would be able to enlighten me about Stu as a kid, growing up in Liverpool. From the outset I got a feeling that this was not going to be the case. Sure enough when I finally got to speak to John I found I was again being interrogated by the family instead of giving me a couple of incidents that happened when they were children. John, an educated man, informed me that he couldn't remember anything except that the young Stuart was quite impish as a little boy, FULL STOP, and the only recollection of that funeral Friday in June 1968 was that the flowers on the coffin were made in the design of a racing car. Unfortunately I had forgotten that detail. What I remember is that I found it extremely difficult to even look at the coffin in the hearse when it pulled up outside 195 Queen's Drive, on that summer's day.

Andrew told me that after the funeral an obituary was in the Liverpool echo. For many weeks later they were receiving mail addressed to the cortege at 195 Queen's Drive, which is extraordinary but then I know that there has always been something extremely foreboding about that house from the shadow over the elegant stairwell to the gravestones that were placed behind the large marble fireplace in the hall. It would be of great interest to all concerned, I believe, to know the history of 195 Queen's Drive, especially for me, having such a unique association with this strange, foreboding house.

Pre-ordained destiny in my life, very much a young lady, Patricia Jackson, that's who I was in June 1968. It took many years to accept the fact that you cannot side step what is meant to be. The realization came from my psychic premonition awareness for the preparation of the unnecessary and all-avoidable fatality of Stu Howitt on that blackest of days in my life.

The only positive thing to come out of this disaster, well, two things really, on the 15th of June 1968 reality made me connect and use my sixth sense awareness from then on. More so than ever before which has been an enormous strength and guide in a life less ordinary, and secondly, I can say to rekindle and reflect those tender spectacular loving times we had, albeit short-lived. Being able to return in my Time Capsule to those glory days when Liverpool was where it was at, beautiful people everywhere, creativity abound on every corner of Liverpool's unique compact city, together with the sixties icons, architecture, individuality, music, sports, religion, two cathedrals either end of a street called Hope, fashion, but above all its genuine good-hearted down to earth, no nonsense people. Real true grit, that's Liverpool and its people. With Stu Howitt fast becoming a champion in his home town at that time in Liverpool's own richness and fame as the history books will tell of Liverpool in all its glory in the sixties.

St Tropez must have been the most favourite of places Stu Howitt had travelled to, although he didn't refer to his trips on his father's boat to St Tropez too much to me. This timeless magic place since the 20th century has been devoid of ostentation, with great panache, beauty and order. Too beautiful to be real! Understandable why he loved this haven! Different, that's the key for me, the individual uniqueness. Even with the glossy hype it remains normal and virtually unchanged for centuries it would appear. He crammed so much into his short life span!

CHAPTER ELEVEN
SYMBOLS

It is written in ancient Eastern Astrology that the symbolic sign of the Horse would abandon everything for "Love". The Horse – a good man and true. He always looks terrific. The horse, quote, with plenty of sex appeal and he certainly knows how to dress, who adores anything where there is plenty of people, concerts, theatres, meetings, sporting occasions, parties, the lot. A sportsman of some note, in general the Horse is gifted, unique. That was the Stu Howitt I knew and loved combined with the Western Astrological sun sign of Taurus the Bull. This combination would be less egotistical of all the combinations of East and West astrological signs of the Horse and the Bull. Wrap it up. I will take it!! What a "Hunk of Guy."

Stu Howitt gave me such respect with a tender loving heart. Which I will keep locked "in my heart forever". He only ever had one other love affair, with Ingrid, to whom he was engaged for two and a half years before he met me. Having now acquired a much deeper insight and analysis throughout the past thirty-nine years I would speculate and state that if we would have been together we would have lived in another place other than Liverpool, probably abroad for half the year and then London based, maybe? But definitely we would have owned a horse or two, there's no question of that. What a dream! Like me Stu was way ahead of his time, sophisticated and true. With all the earthiness of the positive traits of two Earth Sun signs, Taurus and Virgo.

If anyone should ask me what I have done with this Life Less Ordinary, quite simply I have taken care of the people I love and those who have sought my guidance that I have met and known along the highway of my life. God only knows that I have done my best for them and will continue to do so with God's help. Family, husbands, associates and friends. What else are we here for other than to learn and love and help one another, and if we are lucky enough to progress. But it does not always turn out like that, no matter what you do. Here comes that word again: "Destiny." If life were so simplified! IF ONLY.

Since my first date with "Destiny" all those years ago, which I feel changed the true course of my life with the irreplaceable Stuart Howitt, lost and gone forever, I am certain this was the tragedy waiting to happen in my life. Why should I become aware of 195 Queen's Drive in my "Dream Premonition" from that very young age, otherwise? What other reason could there possibly be, to have prior insight and awareness of that day on that funeral Friday in June 1968. The Dream Premonition was quite simply a preparation of my Destiny in a Life Less Ordinary.

July 28th, 1986, a Saturday, in St John's Wood Road, in London, was another extraordinary day. in my Life Less Ordinary. I believe that the presence of the late Stu Howitt saved me from a near fatal car crash on that hot summer evening, with the late Peter Bailey in the driving seat.

This cat lost one of my nine lives in July 1986. I had been unable to sleep the whole night through the night before the car crash. Memories of Stu, feelings swamped me, so vivid, so real. The impact so great and that tranquility that Stu Howitt's effect always had on me, which runs throughout the Howitt family, they all possess this unusual gift. This impact of calm and peace continued throughout that Saturday. I hardly spoke to Peter, which was due to the trance stance that I was in, and did not react with my usual quick response or actions.

We had driven up to St John's Wood Road to look at a flat in Cunningham Place. Just as we were to turn right into the road I noticed a dark coloured car coming towards us from the left, travelling far too fast. I moved in such a slow motion way looking back towards Peter in the driving seat, unable to speak and tell him of this car which was so near and getting nearer. I looked back a second time. I remember thinking: this is it and I don't care anymore. Still unable to speak to Peter Bailey. The car was old and unable to move off quickly, which was fortunate, otherwise the dark coloured vehicle would have hit us, colliding into the passenger door where I was sitting. Just then Peter moved the front of the car trying to make a right turn into Cunningham Place when the other car hit the front of our vehicle with a full-on impact fortunately to the engine of our car.

The other driver ran to our car shouting what's this all about. Peter's voice was raised telling me we could do without this, before getting out of the car, leaving me inside the car. I was still in a trance, but just then a group of people came over to me calling to me to get out the car as it could blow up. At that point when I sat looking across at the car crash did the trance state leave me. When I started to cry. The huge bang and impact could be heard all over the area. As we discovered a couple of years later when we went to view another property in the same building in Cunningham Place. The people who owned the flat remembered us in the car accident and spoke of the huge bang on impact.

So I know Stu saved me from that horrendous car crash in 1986.

CHAPTER TWELVE
THE TRUTH NEVER CHANGES

They say that the greatest gift an author can possess is to write a story from the past as though it was living in the present. I have done my best to create this in my Dream Premonition in Life Less Ordinary and Bailey's Raw Deal. In that precise way in so doing travelling back in my time capsule has released me from my present day burdens and difficulties. It brought me back to days long gone, but still fresh in my emotional psyche, the tenderness and hopeful expectation of life that I had then. I have relived and extracted every ounce of joy and happiness from my past, that is possible in reliving and remembering our "Romantic Association" when Liverpool was at its best and I still had my magnanimous, wonderful Nan to go home to, who understood me so well, God bless my Nan. Everything changes and everything stays the same. Paradoxically there is no such thing as coincidence. Everything happens for a reason.

Olive Howitt had great style, and dignity, ultra ambitious and the driving force of the Howitt family, and their Business ventures. Business acumen second to none! A good mother! My mother believes she would not have let Stuart marry anyone, but I feel she wanted a business arranged marriage to someone extremely wealthy to match their own escalating finances and status and lifestyle, for her beloved son Stuart.

When I started to write this true story I was under the misapprehension that Stu Howitt had attended Quarry Bank Grammar School. Apparently this is not the case. It took Andrew over two years to inform me of that all important fact. I was delighted to learn that he had left school at fifteen just like I did and went on to serve a two year apprenticeship as a tool maker for A. C. Delco, a metal manufacturing company in Edge Lane, Liverpool. Obviously, the Howitts had still to make their money which was not apparent at the time in Stu's teenage years. And more than likely the reason for the long gaps in between Olive Howitt's pregnancies, Stuart was born in 1942, Andrew in 1954, Jonathan 1959, lack of money and prospects when Stu was growing up and then the sudden change of "Good Fortune" in the finances and lifestyle.

When and how this change occurred I do not know, nor have I enquired or been given an insight into their highly improved lifestyle. Apart from hard work and business projects big and small there is the "secret" of their escalation into an extremely affluent lifestyle. Perhaps this could be the reason for the persistent doubting of my reasons for writing my true story of my lifelong passion and love for their older brother. The consistent questioning from the start with Andrew, then Jonathan to a lesser degree, and subsequently, their cousin John Tierl. Which, got to me.

The whole purpose in my writing this unusual story is to remember just how unique Stu Howitt was in so many respects and for his brothers and family to talk of him, as he was .One of Liverpool's outstanding sons.

At least Olive was spared from witnessing the huge trauma of her middle son Andrew's cancer and the hit and run disaster of her daughter-in-law Jean Howitt being killed in June 2006. Davina Howitt, daughter of Jean and Andrew, I'm told is trying to take care of Andrew's business venture in Spain as well as coming to terms with the great loss of her mother, Jean's fatal accident, which is less than a year ago, and this unexpected trauma of her father, Andrew's cancer of the mouth, all this trauma and great loss, at her young age of twenty-three years.The Howitt tragedies continue.

Both Andrew and Jonathan were privately educated at the Liverpool Boys College in Allerton from the age of seven, right through to eighteen. That said, I have to say that neither one of them has the talent, sophistication, and great determination and charisma of their older brother Stuart. Which I am sure they would agree. One of the few questions I ever asked Stu was what school he went to? I understand his reason for the white lie about Quarry Bank School, which was the same as my reason for the lie about still living at Hunt's Cross and not Shiel Park, exactly the same reason.

It's so important for me as it should be for the Howitts to do this for Stuart. I have now completed that all important task which Fate had mapped out for me in 1968. The purpose is complete as it was pre-ordained in my Dream

Premonition. To write about him so he will not be forgotten. Long live the memory of Stuart Duncan Howitt.

Had it not been for Terence Stamp and my association with the world-famous matinee idol when I first arrived in London in 1981 I probably would not have attempted to write anything ever in my life. Stamp inspired me, so I have him to thank for that compliment and inspiration that I can "certainly write" unquote. Stamp was my hero for the first ten years of living in London which helped pull me through some very difficult times with the late Peter Bailey in London in the 1980s. Stamp gave me the all-important CONFIDENCE that I lacked. Everything happens for a reason.

This has to be the final curtain in my long love affair with Stu Howitt. I have to complete the rest of my Destiny and purpose for my lifespan. Because he is not coming back for me, although I know he would have sooner or later given the chance and time. I love you, Stuart. But then I always did, and always will. I will be forever glad and so grateful that we met, albeit too brief an encounter, but all enduring, the ravages of time, "A True Love" which has lasted forty years. Unique! You will be for ever on my mind.

Olive&Joe Howitts Wedding in Liverpool, 1941

CHAPTER THIRTEEN
DESTINATION

A few weeks before the anniversary of the 15th of June 2007, the 39th anniversary of the day Stu Howitt met his tragic untimely end at Oulton Park Race Track. From humble beginnings Stuart was a true star, in the ascendant a real working "class hero". Having now finally been able, to have had a complete insight, into Stu's life and the Howitt family, with my recent meeting with Jonathan and his wife Helen, at the Crowne Plaza hotel in Liverpool. It was during this meeting at the Crowne Plaza hotel, on a Bank Holiday weekend in May 2007, when I had great difficulty to express, how much, and what it meant to me, seeing the whole of Stu's lifespan through these wonderful photographs. Starting with the beautiful Wedding picture of his Mother and Fathers Wedding day, they look so elegant and beautiful. I never expected this unexpected honour. How fantastic was that after 39 years, Spectacular! Jonathan had brought two large bag's full of, old black- and white photo albums of his family. Until this time I was unaware that Jonathan's two young sons were twins, Stuart and Jamie, who are aspiring to become Actors.

Being able to absorb Stu Howitts life and character from the photographic moments in his magical, albeit, brief stay on the Planet, that Stu was a Maverick standing tall, yet alone and with a degree of melancholy about him. Which I could totally identify with, no denying that fact! Looking at him as a boy and throughout his short lifetime was PRICELESS to me!

It was well worth the wait of 39 years, better late then never! Just two weeks before the 39th anniversary June 15th 2007. Olive Howitt had great style, just like Stu, so elegant. She could have become a Model or an Actress. A true grit Liverpudlian who would stand up to her Glaswegian in-laws' and tell them what she thought of them when and if she needed to. Olive was a Smoker all her life which was quite common in those days, especially for Northern Bells! Joe Howitt was such as handsome man when he married Olive. The Wedding photograph says it all about them! I felt so privileged to look through the "Window of their lives"

from those unique pictures of Stu and his family. There was
something so special about this complete insight into this
families history, after all those years. And if I needed any
further confirmation about my preordained destiny which
was waiting at the Cabin Club in January 1968, it was to be
found, on this magical May day, when Jonathan revealed, it
was only 4 years earlier that his brother Stuart had held his
21st Birthday party, at the Cabin Club, with the ever elegant
and glamorous, Olive standing right alongside her beloved
son Stuart. This was no coincidence, when I first met Stu, at
the Cabin Club, this was his Club. It was MEANT TO
HAPPEN!

The Howitt families wealth can only be matched by their
scale of misfortune and tragedy that has befallen them!
Jonathan, put it succinctly when speculating about his older
brother's life. What might have been, had Stu lived. How he
may have worked for Stuart in his business empire or Stuart
may have ended up going Bankrupt, he said. He might even
have ended up hating Stuart. Who knows? Unquote.

And as for me, I would say IF WE ONLY HAD TIME. God
only knows how things may have worked out for Stu and
me. I will continue to cherish Stu Howitts memory for ever.
We will never know, what might have been, given the
chance and the time. IF ONLY…

Stuart Howitts, 21st Birthday at the Cabin Club May 15th
1964, Liverpool, with his Mum and Dad